Witness

By Adam E. Holton

Self-published 2024 by Adam E. Holton
Copyright © Adam E. Holton, 2024
Music Copyright © Hieronymus Peach, 2024
Cover Design Copyright © Sophie Jones, 2024

The right of Adam E. Holton to be identified as the author and self-publisher of this work has been asserted by him in accordance with Copyright, Designs and Patents Act 1988.

All rights reserved. No part of this publication may be reproduced, stored in a retrieval system, or transmitted, in any form, or by any means (electronic, mechanical, photocopying, recording or otherwise) without the prior written permission of the author.

ISBN: 978-3-9519673-0-1

This is a work of narrative philosophy and combines elements of real life and fiction. Any resemblance to actual persons, living or dead, events or places where permission was not possible have been changed to respect the livelihoods and autonomy of those people.

Printed and bound by Tiskárna PROTISK s.r.o. Czech Republic.
Tiskárna PROTISK s.r.o. Rudolfovská 617, České Budějovice 370 01
Tel.: 386 360 136 www.protiskcb.cz

This book is sold subject to the condition that it shall not, by way of trade or otherwise, be lent, hired out, or otherwise circulated without the author's prior consent in any form of binding or cover or other than that which it is published and without a similar condition including this condition being imposed on the subsequent purchaser.

Contact for author: Adam E. Holton   adam@foundoutthere.com

Contact for composer: Hieronymus Peach   Only by word of mouth

For more information visit foundoutthere.com

Thanks to my family for life.

Thanks to S. & D. for their patience and support.

Thanks to the people of l'Asilo for giving me a place to dream.

Herein

Prologue

1   *December 5th 2021*

2   *First coffee of the day*

3   *Moody and Mindful*

4   *Meraviglioso*

5   *Second coffee and conjuring*

6   *Welsh Solitaire*

7   *Remember*

8   *A palm for a sole*

       Intermission for hands

9   *A Keaton Step*

       Intermission for feet

10   *Dry socks and monologues*

Intermission for tongues

11 *Focaccia for you and sweeping*

12 *To myself*

13 *Perhaps*

14 *Jellyfish. Chess. Ljubljana. Luka.*

Intermission for eyes

15 *Juggling birds of sand*

Intermission for ears

16 *Will you allow me the pleasure of disappearing?*

17 *Can you see their faces?*

Epilogue

This novel is accompanied by a few pieces of music. Follow the link below to listen:

"Vuttamme e'mmane!"

**Neapolitan saying, roughly translated as
'throw out your hands and get involved'**

Enter a Ship-Master and a Boatswain

Ship-Master	*Boatswain!*
Boatswain	*Here, master: what cheer?*
Ship-Master	*Good, speak to the mariners: fall to't yarely, or we run ourselves a-ground, bestir, bestir.*

The Tempest, Act 1 Scene 1

Prologue

In this moment I wish only to be where my arse is right now.

Here. Here and now. Being here. Now. I breathe in so deep I can taste the salt in the wind.

If I shuffle around a little I can feel the cold in the stone of the harbour wall beneath me. I push my palms down. The rough-hewn slabs are carved out of the boulder thrown at Odysseus by the cyclops on Mongibello. Or so some say. I exhale.

I want to focus on the sound of the waters in the strait of Messina. I look up and watch the glare of a spotlight catching the face of the Madonna della Lettera. She observes the water as well, humming and murmuring poetry and prayers for those at sea tonight.

I notice I am mumbling too. Do I have any words for myself? What would I say in the face of nature? Would I be humble or a nuisance?

I put my palms to my stomach, cushioning my diaphragm. I breathe in. Slow through my nose, gathering in a lungful.

I do not wish to look behind me. I am longing to witness life anew.

I pause. I remember. I wish only to be where my arse is right now. I exhale. I wonder.

I wonder what I would have felt if the hallowed auditorium of the Vittorio Emanuele theatre had been full of laughter, mirth and mischief. Would I feel relieved? Rejuvenated?

Would I have felt catharsis?

I wonder.

From what depths would my laughter have risen? Would I have felt closer to the strangers around me? I wonder what this last half an hour on Sicily would have felt like if I had been well humoured.

I wonder.

I breathe in. Slow. Allowing the ghost sounds of laughter remembered to be collected by my wilful thoughts. Letting them enter the thought stream. Teasing their way into the blood stream.

Somewhen in the performance, when all was going to shit, a person a few rows in front of me shuffled around as the incessant noises grew to an uncomfortable, cacophonous pitch. The noises stopped for a single, measured beat. And somehow, through the divine comedy of existence, that person a few rows ahead of me set free a fart of such resonance that some of us close enough to hear got to laugh. I wonder if they heard it in the upper circle seats. Did they hear it in the Gods?

I wonder. I breathe out. This time a little easier. I let the air flow through me.

I push my hands down again. Perhaps it's time to move. I hear a bell nearby begin and call out midnight. I have half an hour to board the train. A juvenile excitement seizes me. The train rolls onto a ferry to cross the strait before we head to Naples on my way to Slovenija. A boat train. I love travelling by train.

I feel a little better now, but I doubt that was the last wave of sadness to come through me. I realise I'm longing for people's fascination with doom to be replaced by the humour in resilience; an ability to recognise the wonderous in the ordinary, unfurling moments of life. Stories that endear me, to help me endeavour; that remind me to listen and to persevere.

I wonder which stories I would share.

I stretch my hands up, a comic imitation of the Madonna, and sing a humane prayer for my own crossing; a cry that mingles with the breathy song of the midnight waters. I clap my hands to summon the will to carry on. I walk towards the station, my feet a little damp, these shoes are not in such good condition, but they are all I have for now. At least I am still entertained by my own circumstances.

I wonder how we learn to laugh. I wonder what first set me off? When did my humour become so visceral?

I wonder.

When did I learn to let a stranger make me laugh?

Do ducks laugh at the wind?

Is there ever really a last laugh?

I wonder.

I walk towards Messina Centrale to catch a train heading north.

1   December 5th 2021

This morning it is raining on Piazza Bellini and, as I breathe in – watching the leaves grow from the slumbering trees, dreams from the dead teased out by warm winds, on via Santa Maria di Costantinopoli – I realise I love life today for the melodies her existence makes; especially the ones I cannot hear.

Somehow I have taught myself to allow the rain to inspire a ruthless optimism in me. A wilful, determined resilience. I love it as the rain falls. I wonder if it will continue all day until I catch my train to the north.

In this moment, I also find myself wondering if I am perhaps wearing the wrong shoes for Piazza Bellini in December. Dancehall soles, suitable for celebrations not cobbles. Old leather for young feet. A few more holes than are helpful.

I often feel like I'm wearing the wrong shoes, or at least, I feel like a birch tree standing in the middle of an opera house – with all its well-heeled and well-oiled patrons clambering around, demanding that I be moved elsewhere.

I look up at the statue of Vincenzo Bellini. I wonder what he did when he had wet feet.

A waitress appears from the doorway over there. She begins to bring out tables, unfolding them slowly; careful not to trap her fingers in the metal joints.

I'm still a little sad after the show last night. I had hoped a ballet at the Vittorio Emanuele would have given me solace or mirth. But I was mistaken. Five minutes in and all the dancers were being shot. The music was deafening. The dancers came back as zombies and violently threw themselves around the stage as political speeches became part of the music. Then there was an explosion. Then it ended. The programme described it as 'an exploration of the future for society'.

Some days I feel an incomprehensible misery of questions. In other moments, I feel more confused; bewildered. I struggle to believe that repeating violence, reflecting it back at a captive audience is really what people want to express in the pursuit of living, especially in the houses of the arts.

With all the horror in this epoch of change, I would love to make a grave for greed, despair and resignation. I would love to learn how to dream of life being otherwise. I would love to learn of how other people dream of life being different. I long to hear about it so I may move towards it. I wish someone would tell me how it smells, what they see there, what sounds live there.

I hear someone sneeze in the square. I look towards the eruption and see a man crossing towards the little alley that leads to Piazza Dante. He's dressed in old academic robes and wears a dishevelled mortarboard upon his head. He wipes his nose and rights himself. Wedged beneath his armpits are giant cards with elaborate mathematical sums on them, equations that mean nothing to me. I stare as he takes his first step into the street.

When I was on Sicily, I heard stories about a street performer whose art is his mental capacity to calculate any sum asked of him, without any assistance, and provide the answer; whereupon the audience is invited to check his answer and verify his accuracy. Defiance has as many forms as intelligence.

He takes a second step. I feel the storm's breath push past me, kissing me lightly on the cheek as it rushes towards him. The wind hits him midstride and although he doesn't fall, he is blown apart. His trestle table crashes to the street. His sums are scattered and cast about like feathers before they fall. His hat teeters above his eyes, but does not abandon him.

He stands still, the rain continuing to wash his robes. He looks towards the mouth of the alley. Before he has chance to lower his head, before he swears, before the wind howls again, a loud, warm voice calls out to him.

His guardians arrive, also wet. Three strangers have gathered up his affects and approach him. They make a small comedy of tucking them back under his armpits. One goes so far as to right his cap and pull it down a little. His table is also returned. The four of them stand beneath the rain. Some words are shared that I cannot hear.

The strangers depart.

The mathematician stands a moment longer before carrying on his way and disappears into the alley. It doesn't always have to be so difficult; it's not all a riddle.

I hear the whine of more metal tables being unfolded somewhere else, but their complaint is a little quieter now.

It is early morning in the square. The cobbles are wet, they glisten like irises blown through with light; shimmering lakes reflecting chalk mountains.

I behold the rising murmurs of the dawn ensemble, observe the imagined shadows dancing across the buildings; each as graceful as their circumstance allows. Meandering tenants plumbing a path. Stalking merchants balancing clasped fists. Traffic conductors floundering like aged vultures. Mothers casting limbs aloft like luminaries as their children disperse into the city.

I feel the small flame at the base of my spine, kindled in my coccyx; the one that carries me forth. I would love a companion's ear, a stranger's ear in this time between trains. Ah, to be heard.

A person walks past me as I swim in these thoughts.

It's Valeria! A friend from elsewhere. She's up early. What's she doing here in Naples? I chase after her, but I'm mistaken. They turn around and I see another face. "Pardon me," I shout. "I'm tired."

I am tired.

Perhaps I'll perch here a while on the stone steps beneath the statue. I do not mind the rain, it is not so heavy now. Look, you can almost see up Vincenzo's nose from this angle. I'll watch the people a while as I figure this day out.

-

This one, massaging the air with her palms, drawing soft patterns with her fingertips.

That one warming their hands in the pockets of their coat. Their musing entertains them, look how they grin.

This one, singing a lullaby to the sky, the remains of the morning rain clinging to her shoulders in the fibres of a loose jacket. She looks unconcerned by the fresh wind teasing the collar into a dance only tailors can name.

That one needs the toilet.

This one's reciting Dante as he waits for the lights to change.

They have enough maps to make a mess of the directions. I hope they have the time to walk slowly.

This one watches me. I attempt to put on my gloves, cold as it is. I laugh at myself as the bundle of wool and stitches drifts into a puddle. She sees it too. She smiles at me as our eyes meet. I feel giddy, I feel joyous. I feel silly – as if I'm running about someone else's house in only my underwear on a Saturday morning before sunrise, searching for everything and nothing. I feel intimate, enveloped, a blossom or a leaf in the wind, as she shares her smile with me. I feel relief. I feel my tensions unravel a little more. I think, perhaps, I'll bow to her in awe. I smile in return, to her expression; perhaps we are only watching each other.

I feel naïve, curious – watching a mountain river find its path anew through winter's debris.

Who am I without you? Who are we without one another? Distraction swallows me whole.

2   *First coffee of the day*

Shibanyatsi! Another puddle for these holes. My foot slips and I find an ocean. And again, this ache in my back. I am wearing the wrong shoes for Piazza Bellini this morning.

I know, a coffee. I'll try in there.

In the corner of this café, there is a piano. I choose to sit there, on the stool, only for a brief moment. As I sit at the piano, I am told it belonged to Totò. I consider playing a song about a man running down a mountain to warm his feet. I dream of a fisherman's' collarbones as my fingers wash over the white keys and the black in equal measures, tracing good humour and time as if it were so real that we could chase it to make others laugh. I decide to release a different piece[1] into the morning, of a lady who was brave enough to listen, to look.

I feel someone watching me. I look up as I play. They are on the other side of the window. I think of the damp-cold that blushes their feet in those old shoes they wear. I smell a strong coffee and the sweetness of a pistachio cream cornetti sail past.

---

[1] Valeria's Tears on the Witness EP. See link on *Herein* pages.

I heard that a lazy waiter has fine smelling fingers because they use them to pick up the pastries. If you were to hold them up to your nose you would smell almonds and oranges, blueberry nails. I would hold one up to my nose so I could inhale it, perhaps imbibe their symphony a little closer so my memory could describe them deeper into its library (atlas?). Ah, I yearn for such sensuality, but which waiter here would let me sniff their fingers?

I look up again, the window is empty glass and distant brick. I look at Totò's piano once more.

I hear a familiar sound in the café near Piazza Bellini. I turn around on the piano stool. A waiter is staring at me. They do not look like the lazy type. I blush at them. But I hold their gaze, showing them my embarrassment and I know it's OK to do so, to be so, to have so – comfortable as I am in the warmth, forgetting the ache in my spine that runs into my knees.

I order something in patchwork Italian. They don't know what I've been thinking, but it takes me a breath cycle to settle myself down, giddy as I am.

I'll rest my legs as I sit at this piano; my right foot balanced on the sustain pedal, pulsing (a river?). And here, I glance about the photos framed and resting across the shoulders of the piano.

I think of Sun Ra. I recall the impossible ourselves, improbable myself, nothing more than a pebble perched on the lip of a magnificent waterfall and, as the river swells, I am pushed and pulled into the cascading dance of water. Sometimes it is alluring, encouraging to believe I could also be an infinite collection of pebbles that arrive on the lip of the waterfall. I could wait afresh in each moment, eager and nervous, loquacious with my peace dreams, waiting for an interaction, for the weave of another conversation.

I long for connection in the being, in the breathy human song; not in the dull intercourse of text messages.

My order arrives.

I hold aloft my desire to be here with a dear stranger. To discuss and share what else has been found out there. What stories have made an impression on us? What phrases, new metaphors, what fine words have been tasted? What new melodies have been sung? I'm keen to hear them. I'm eager to share mine, if only to exhale for a change. To converse through the time between trains.

I drink my first coffee of the day. I leave the piano. I ascend steps to the street and thrust both my hands up into the morning sky, if only as a beacon, beckoning for a stranger to talk with in this ordeal of hide and seek.

I close my eyes as I push my hands further up into the air. It feels like there is water gushing out of my palms and falling over me, but it is only the blood in my veins surrendering to the gesture, retreating from my fingers to my heart, this heart. And I open the corner of my eye. To peak. To look around, hoping to see someone, but instead my eye closes itself, drawn shut by a dream, and I let my reminiscences sing to me.

Memories and reveries distend awhile, unfurling experiences of being otherwise. But without enough nourishment they distort themselves, becoming sticky, oil-stained sand. I decide to pull up the cobbles of these streets, and fold the avenues and the cornices of gothic terrace houses, awnings of skies woven beyond mountains, curves of rivers, wings of heron, the limbs of each tree I have ever climbed to preserve them before they are ruined by tarry doubt. I ball these wonders into a single marble of thought.

I turn it, this seed, slow in the axis of my mind's embrace, and wait. Outside my dreaming, my feet burn with cold, exquisite breathes that lope and sear across the canvas of my skin.

These are not the right shoes for Piazza Bellini.

These doubts, that I tell myself, I do not blame myself for conjuring them. What else do they point towards? What do they suggest? Is my doubt a mispronounced longing for comfort, for the familiar, for awe? If we only practice expressing what we don't want, where do we learn to communicate what we need?

When I notice what I'm longing for I rub this marble until it disappears. The flourish of realisation, of relief is tangible in my blood, electric seams weaving the tapestry of my essence. I long for company. I don't not want to harden myself within a mosaic of coarsened fears; worries of being lonely today in Naples.

In this sense of relief, I raise myself up, celebrating the death of this minor fear, dancing as if barefoot across the shimmering

coals, glittering and raw. I sing a sonnet for *satyagraha* and find
a nest for my recollections of joy.

In the darkness of my musing, I feel the generous, playful kiss
of renewed rains, *return to me,* the kinky humour of existence
in the benevolence of water itself that covers my face, my eyes,
the archipelagos of lost hours, the spirit of my flesh. I turn my
arms in the vibrant air and thrust them up further into the sky;
deeper into the firmament.

I open both eyes into the nascent storm. Winter in Naples
brings the monsoons. I cast my gaze about and find the street. I
find myself here, here again. Just around the corner from Piazza
Bellini, on the street that leads to the theatre named after
Vincenzo. I am nourished by the death of my dreaming.

Yet still, I am a little tired.

I pull my fingers down from the sky, painted by the first rains,
and stuff them, tuck them into my pockets. I am hungry now,
and I feel a little delinquent. I had better conjure a remedy or
else step inside somewhere for a moment to eat.

I will go in here. There are not so many lights and I can see a man dressed as a waiter, folding napkins into a chest. In the corner of the mirror on the wall behind him I spy another piano. I am fated it seems. A moment please. I search for the words to begin the morning in a language that is not my first tongue.

3   Moody and Mindful

As I rummage around for the words, I peer outside. I see only the trees. I get tangled between my translations and my meandering humours.

—

Have you ever noticed, there can be a dialogue when it comes to hunger? One voice, mindful of my needs, urging myself towards eating, but then the other, the moody bastard, intervenes and protests with another reason why you should put it off for a little longer. Why I can't always get them to sit down together I don't know. And the uncertainty makes me smile. Sometimes it makes me confused, but makes me glad I have a choice some days. In this moment, the voices, sadly, do not agree:

Moody: I am tired. I can't look after myself at the moment. I am shaking, I'm vibrating! This can't be right. It carries on.

Mindful: The food will revive you, if you let it. Please, begin.

Moody: I'm not sure I can, not right now, but perhaps in a little while.

> It falls sullen for a moment, but flares up again

Look at my lips. I know I can't continue this way, but for now I'm too delicate. I don't even know what my organs could withstand. I, I. I just want to look. To see. To witness this morning. Look at all these people. Can't we stand out there for a moment?

> So, the thoughts and their voices step outside, leaving me dumb and bereft in the face of the waiter. They are unconcerned about me. They have other things to discuss.

Moody: Here, here are all these people. There are more people here on this one street in Naples than I have ever seen in all my dreams. It is so. You may think it unlikely, but I am not so much of a dreamer. I did not learn how to dream until much later. Until more recently I mean.

> If thoughts could look, they would cast their eyes about the scene.

If I stand here, I can smell the rough edges and the rinds of parmigiano next to a glass of red wine. I can see into that man's throat as he shows his palate to his wife, or is it his sister, or his mother, or auntie. She illuminates it with a light source on a mobile phone. I can see the coffee scum on his tonsils! And, this lady is rummaging in her bag, for what, I will never know.

> At this point the other voice attempts to divert the conversation, but is thwarted by the petty profundity spewing out of the first.

Moody: But I feel curious. Not that I want to look inside her bag. Not really.

Mindful: You know, to become aroused by curiosity is enough, sometimes. Do you fancy choosing something to...

Moody: No! The crowd sways along the flagstone street, undulating, oscillating between steps and surprises, between scents and, no! I don't want to go that way. Leave me alone. See, I am too delicate to be out here. If you want to carry on your search let me alone. Please. I want to eat, but I don't want it now. Please, just a little while longer, to rest, to figure it out.

Mindful: Figure what out? They only have cornetti at this hour. Perhaps you've had too much coffee on an empty stomach.

Moody: NO! (pause) Perhaps.

But I digress.

I cannot express this as I figure out what to say to the waiter. He smiles, points to a place where I can sit and says he'll bring me something. There are some faces everyone understands.

4   *Meraviglioso*

Some days I want to dream only through and with my ears. To become entranced by a movement played on an instrument with no name. To audiate. To compose dream-sounds, synaesthesia as a verb. To synaesthesise out of the ghosts of stimuli that dance among the burping geysers of my memories, as if these figments were sketched from the landscapes of place I have never been, the impressions I have gathered, perceptions conceived of intuitions.

Perhaps the aspiration to see such a place for myself one day is what makes my descriptions more fanciful, rendered magnificent by the yearning for such a home. It takes a while to remember it doesn't live on the other side of a gulf, this longing. It isn't a disparate, desperate illusion. If I sang to it, if I sang for a home, we would be drawn together. Somehow. Somewhen. Of that, I am sure.

You know, if we sang to life, I wonder how long before we realise there are over eight billion versions of the truth alive. Isn't that fascinating? And imagine if they could coexist and interact. At peace in difference. Wouldn't that be something marvellous. I love that word. I've even learnt it in Italian. *Meraviglioso*. Love a good marvel in the morning. Would that there was world enough and time.

5   *Second coffee and conjuring*

The waiter puts down a pistachio cornetti, an espresso and a glass of water. I'll begin with the glass of water. I've already had coffee this morning. I contemplate the cup, the steam flavouring the air. I wonder what I could do with it if you were here. Would you want my coffee?

I imagine you are sat here with me.

I become a little nervous, excited perhaps. While you decide whether to have the coffee or not, I allow my sensations, other recollections, to carry me off on the choir breath of a sea-change sung heart.

I dream of a place where you could be. I conjure tastes and sounds that accompany you. I consider a path you have taken to be here with me now.

I realise my eyes have closed.

I am relieved to find you still deciding when I open them.

Such wandering thoughts fill me with a kind of beautiful sorrow and a playfulness. I let the thought die. I breathe out.

I sit up. Just a moment, I want to rearrange myself on the chair. I look out the window. I gaze at the rooftops. I think the sky looks a milky-grey. I feel calm. There is a familiar lull, a pause, unbroken by concerns and buoyed by the occasional babble of the people beyond the window and the new people arriving.

More questions emerge and unfurl, arise and spill, climb and hoist themselves towards my lips. I breathe in. I enjoy how my eyes move, shivering a little as they dream of you. I wait.

I would love to tell you about someone I met earlier on.

6   *Welsh Solitaire*

There was a lady on the train from Sicily.

I have a habit of bemoaning the fates of modern train passengers. It is an inner monologue, an ongoing complaint. What I don't understand is how someone could own a train company who clearly gives so little thought to the comfort of other people. Some of the new carriages don't even have tables.

But I digress.

I'm glad they sent the older carriages to Sicily. The ones with tables. I sat at one in Messina this morning, not seven hours ago. I was alone at the table for most of the journey, sat with a cabaret of revelations in my thoughts provoked by that dismal performance from the night before.

I heard the clamour of dawn passengers ascending at Salerno. The pale reflection of a young lady stood in the window, wearing an unusual, double breasted polo coat and furry bucket hat with the brim rolled up. Aura of bustling intent, bouquet of morning coffee in the twilight. I wondered what she was travelling towards.

She put down a stained and dented travelling cup on the table, ink on her fingertips. She settled herself into the chair opposite me, sighing steam onto the cold glass. Once content, she plucked a deck of emerald-backed playing cards from an inside pocket and laid out a peculiar tableau of solitaire. I followed each flourish as she raised a card before her, watched each dedication as she placed the card on the table and reached for the next. The difference in the arrangement encouraged me to fumble through my Italian, to ask, to appeal for understanding.

"*Solitaire Cymreig*. Welsh Solitaire," she replied. "Want to learn?"

"Why not?" I conjured from within, opening up towards a chance lesson. I revelled in how refreshing the distraction felt after the disappointment of the night before.

"I can teach you before we arrive in Naples where I leave you."

I nodded, understanding enough and sit forward as she

reshuffled the cards. She split them into a crude half deck and began talking to me as she gave me one of the stacks. I focussed on her hands, watching the unadorned surface of the table. Nothing happened.

I looked up; she was waiting. Our eyes met. We breathed. I think she recognised that I am still learning her language. She looked at the cards and then at me again. She nodded. I nodded, and encountered an uncanny thought encouraging me, urging me to mimic her.

I placed my half in the mirror hand to hers. She nodded again and laughed, a sound both blithe and jocose that helped me feel secure, reassured. Perhaps we understood one another.

Each card she pulled from the stack was accompanied by an embellished gesture. I replied with my own burlesque. In ascending order from left to right she placed a single card, a pair, a trio a quartet; a quintet to finish the array. She put the remaining cards in a pile above the longest column.

She picked up the lone card, pulled up to her chest, and peeked at it with a giddy enthusiasm. She laid it down face up, exposed on the table in its original place. I mimicked her. We exposed the bottom card of each column with playful significance.

She pulled the top card from each of the remaining stacks and laid it face up. She gestured one up, one down and played out a couple cards from her array. She reached an impasse, drew both hands away from the cards and we both grinned. She picked another card from the top. I brought my hands from the edge of the table back towards the cards and she nodded.

"When all cards are on the table, you touch the smallest pile," she slammed her hand down on the space beside the cards, "and we start again. It ends when you have no cards left, when you have given everything away."

"*Regala tutto,*" I replied and slammed my own hand down on the table.

She reshuffled, we aligned our cards and we began a round. I noticed her lucid movements, the familiarity of the game. I watched myself fumble and snatch at the cards in a scramble to pick them up as fast as possible. Each time I got close I still brought my hand down on the bigger pile.

"It is ok. Remember, you want to give them away. Only take back the little you need."

There was a practiced impulse behind each lunge she made as her array disappeared. As she picked the next card from her diminished pile, I couldn't help but relish in the peculiar humour of the quickening pace of each round. I felt absorbed and effervescent.

Whilst I was turning over cards, I heard the echo of her hand hitting the bare table. I looked up from the mess before me and found her smiling. For a brief moment our thoughts were nowhere else. We were aware of the chairs, the table, the train, the world outside in an distant sense. But we were there at the table together. Players in an interlude. I breathed out, longing to remember this sense of ease.

The train slowed down. We both glanced out of the window. Naples sprawled and climbed away from us at such bizarre angles, astounding my sense of perspective. I'd never seen the city before. I took the ferry to Palermo from the North.

She swept the cards into a messy pile between her palms. She looked up as she arranged them.

"Can you remember that? I have a spare deck if you'd like one."

"I can try."

"Just remember not to be greedy; no one wants all the cards at the end of the game."

She slid the deck back into the box with a calm confidence. Another deck appeared on the table as I was busy watching her hands. It surprised me. It was held together by an elastic band, wrapped round double. The backs of the cards were a kind of vibrant, ultramarine blue like her coat. Each card had a lighter and darker blush in places, like holding up a fingertip to a lightbulb or to the sun.

She tapped the table.

"There is good coffee in Piazza Bellini if you have time. I should know; they order from me."

She wished me well and disappeared before I could move. It took me a moment to gather myself. I exhaled, oh for the joy of train tables!

We had arrived in Naples, only eleven hours until my next train. There was a blossoming relief within me. I decided to try carrying it towards Piazza Bellini, longing to sustain it; aware that it may falter, reaching for the name of a song only half remembered. I had no bag. I collected my own coat, the cards and wondered how to find Piazza Bellini without a map.

7   *Remember*

When we have forgotten to play, we must remember everything manmade can and will be late, dismissed or abandoned at some point – just like utopia, just like heaven, just like hell, just like war.

In accepting that, all of human kind shows its creative soul. In acknowledging that everything may die, we can present ourselves naked to the ocean of the possible.

Then we may long to play once more.

8   *A palm for a sole*

I show you the deck of cards. I let you play with them; turning them over to admire the design and the colour. I enjoy the calm lull between us. I breathe out when it feels right to carry on.

−

I give in to the dream.

I'm really starting to accept that I don't have the right shoes on. Look at them, they're soaked through. I'm sure I could wring out an ocean if I took them off. And look at yours! You're not doing any better. Both of us. We must laugh at ourselves for something, no?

I've got an idea though, I'm sure it'll help. Show me your hands. Put them here, here like this. A palm for a sole. Imagine a clam. Yes. Hold your hands open like a clam, part teased open please. One moment. Yes.

No, please, don't worry. You don't have to touch my feet. I'm

not going to put my foot in your hands. I'll touch my own.
You touch yours. Unless that's something that interests you.
No?

I can see you smiling though.

Think of a clam. No, I won't touch your feet.

—

I tease one of my feet between my palms.

—

Just for a moment. See, this will help get the blood back into them.

—

And I watch as you take off your sock. I see your hands close around your naked foot and my thoughts begin to drift.

Intermission for hands

I wonder how your hands feel. I wonder about how your fingers interlace. Would you say your hands are strong? Are they delicate? How do the veins and arteries shape the backs of your hands? Have you ever painted them? Do they get cold at the tips? What memories live inside your knuckles?

Are they similar to mine or different?

I wonder how it feels to hold your hands in mine. To stroke the palm of your left hand. What do your fingers taste like? Do you kiss your wrists for good luck? Do people read fingers as well, or just palms?

I used to measure how healthy I was, or mentally sound I was, by how thick my thumbs were.

What stories do your hands tell you?

Would you tell me?

I wonder what your hands have held, carried, cherished, nourished. I wonder what you believe is possible because of your hands.

Have you ever held life in your hands?

How did that feel?

I wonder.

Resume

9   *A Keaton Step*

Do you think they'd let us dry our socks and that radiator? Can you ask in Italian? I can pantomime, but with requests such as this I always tell myself it's better not to ask in English. Thank you.

—

As you return sockless to the table, we both see the flash of lightning from the corner of our eyes. We turn to look out the window. We both see a young woman scuff the toe of her boot on a cobble stone and lurch forward. She catches herself and reasserts her balance, walking out of view; a little slower than before.

—

That tremble, that shuffle and adjustment. We are both a child and a dancer when we stumble. It makes us attentive, refocus, humbled and humoured. A small humiliation can be helpful at times. It distracts us from whatever carried us to such a fate and realigns us. It's true. Falling over. Falling.

That reminds me.

Did you ever hear of a Keaton step? Do you know who Buster Keaton was?

Perhaps he was a bit before your time. Before our time. Born in 1895. I only know a bit about his films. Anyway. He fell over a lot. Made a living out of falling over. He made millions of people laugh because of the ways he fell over.

In his early twenties, he was called up to serve in the American Expeditionary Forces in France; during the First World War. As with a person whose flame can dance in the darkest of nights, he continued to perform vaudeville acts for and with the soldiers. The battalions of men flowed in and ebbed away from the camp, or life. One evening, a band of London lads came upon the show. It left an indelible mark upon the imagination of one in particular.

This one, and a few from his gang, survived the war and made their way home to Bethnal Green. Beleaguered by doubt, time and night terrors, he set out in search of work. This was the era when most men had little space to express what they had endured. Although we were taught of the war poets in school, there were scores, entire orchestras of men made illiterate by suffering and social etiquette.

He took on work as a labourer, with the intention of setting up as a builder himself. Within four short years, due in part to dedication and demand, he set up a small company, surrounded by some of his fellow soldiers. And, of all the ardours of the trade, he felt most proud of his staircases. Couldn't say why they brought him such pride, but was often heard discussing the ratios of a riser, the depth of tread and the comedy of a crooked newel post.

One Friday evening in May of 1924, after finishing a job near Leicester Square, he was kicking stones about the street on his long walk home. A knuckle of earth glanced the wall beside him and he looked up. On the wall was a poster for a new American film. As he looked closer at the face of the protagonist and read the names, he recognised the man from France who even in the midst of war could rouse laughter. He checked his pay packet and decided to skip his usual beer for the chance to see the film.

Later on, as people poured out of the cinema, he watched as the other patrons tripped themselves up, throwing themselves about the steps and into the street in imitation of Mr Keaton. One person in fell beside him and grabbed onto his shoulder, laughing and apologising. He smiled and watched as the stranger walked away, before he turned to his own path and carried on home.

The following Friday he was in the pub with the men he worked with. Sometimes, during the evening, there would be a solemn moment; an atmosphere would envelope the group and each would drink in silence. As one such bout subdued those gathered, he looked outside. He witnessed someone stumble up a short flight of stairs across the street. He chuckled to himself. No one seemed to be hurt and he didn't feel guilty for laughing. He forgot the field of his memories that he had been sliding across and sinking into.

He looked at the men, all deep in their own trenches of thought. As simple as inspiration can be, he interrupted and started to tell them about the film he'd seen the previous week. Thinking as he was talking, he happened upon the idea of building a peculiar pair of steps into every flight. Both would have an equal tread to all the others, but would be different in rise; the first being shallower, the second deeper. A Keaton Step. The slight awakening of someone stumbling out of their reveries and being brought, humble, to the present moment appealed to them; a kind of language in motion that could make real the things they couldn't say themselves. It would be a respite from the echoes of war, caused by what looked like chance.

He set about trying to win them work in public spaces and soon they got a good reputation for working diligently and as quick as the Irish. The jobs came and, in every flight of stairs, they built a Keaton Step. The was no guarantee anything would ever come of it, but they were proud of the mischief they hid within the walkways of London.

Now, if this were a story for our times, it would probably begin with two clean and confused health and safety officers wandering around with cameras, bemoaning the shoddy building of the past. And, as they returned to the office, shouting distraught and belligerent slurs at these unknown workers for burdening them with paperwork and case folders, they would enter their manager's office to complain.

They would sit down and whinge to the older supervisor about these steps and the carelessness of people of the past. He would inquire to see a photo of the steps that were causing such frustration. With a short word he would dismiss their concern. These anomalies were not to be removed. He would turn to them, these learned graduates, and ask whether they knew what a Keaton Step was. When they didn't, he would begin by asking whether they knew who Buster Keaton was, and a myth would be born again, in the hope that laughter will always outlive misery.

Intermission for feet

I wonder how your feet pulse when you're light on your soles. I wonder how your ligaments tense and relent, absorbing each impact. I wonder how they smell after a fortnight of dancing, after a stroll with an intimate spirit, after a sprint to the station. I wonder how they yearn for connection, contact.

I wonder how your arch bows as you adjust to your mercurial and incessant burdens. How do they change as you walk with intent? With purpose? With despair?

I wonder, can you touch your heels? Feeling the weave of where those ligaments and tendons stretch to, where they stretch from.

Do you carry your weight in other ways? Do you carry the weight of others as well? Is the skin callused, rough or soft?

Do you ever rub your bare feet in the earth? In the river? In the sky?

How is walking around barefoot a sign of madness?

Have you ever braved licking your own foot or someone else's?

Would you if you could?

I wonder how you care for your feet? With oils, ointments or intuition?

What do you wish for your feet?

I wonder.

Resume

10   Dry socks and monologues

Perhaps our socks are dry by now. I'll go get them. Perhaps I'll find us some newspaper for stuffing inside our shoes to try and dry them as well. If not, I think I'll leave mine off for a bit. What's the word for socks? *Calzini?* Yes, I'll be back. I've still got plenty of time before my train. It's not until the early evening.

–

I plant my palms on the table and hoist myself up into the room. I am optimistic the socks will be drier. I am content to let simple matters restore me. I feel more buoyant than I did at dawn, though not much has changed.

My concern for the ballet aches less. I hear my humoured heart whisper 'you mar our labour, keep your cabins, you do assist the storm'.

Consider who your words make master before you decide to speak. More speed less haste. You still have a choice. I know where I'd prefer to give my attention.

The cold of the terracotta tiles on my bare feet reminds me of myself, my whole self, as I walk towards the waiter.

The relief of a burden lost, freed from such bitterness, soothes my worrisome soul. I feel therefore I am. Sweet catharsis.

Now, my socks.

—

Dove sono i miei calzini?

—

I love a pair of dry socks. They were in the back. Strange what kindness some people will offer, even so early in the day. Can I offer you something to eat? Surely it is a good time to eat? I will pay for the coffee and go in search of something for us. Please, it would be my pleasure. It's been a good year workwise for a change.

—

As I stand to pay, I find a book in my pocket. I wonder what you'd make of it. If I leave it with you, I could have a bit more time to find us something delicious to eat. Perhaps.

—

Would you like something to read while I'm away? I could leave you with this? It's a play manuscript. I found it on the train coming here. It was on the seat before the lady with the cards arrived. Forgive me, I make notes in the margins and fold page corners. I hope you don't mind. Or would you like to play with the cards? Not yet, ok. Well enjoy the play. I'd be curious to know your thoughts. Then perhaps we'll move and eat? Wonderful. Until soon.

MAN IN WAITING

3 Monologues

BY FRANCESCA QUATTROMANI

Monologue 1:

St. Bruno

Hospital clinic. Hallway waiting area. Three chairs against a wall. Martin Campbell is sat alone on the far-left seat. Early thirties. Male. Tired. Waiting. He squints at the top left of the stage.

Over tannoy: *Herr Ploner, Herr Ploner nach Raum Zwei. Raum Zwei, Herr Ploner.*

Martin watches someone (ghost) pass.

Martin: I'm getting better at listening. And being patient. Well. Not so much better at being patient. But I do have a new word today. *Hebamme. Hebamme. Hebamme. Wo ist die Hebamme?* Sounds like an 80s loincloth cartoon hero. *HEBAMME!*

Hebamme means midwife in German.

It's hard trying to learn a new language as you're going along. I've got some questions for the midwife, but I hope she's patient with me. I got on fine for a while because everyone kept talking in English to me. Never got a chance to practice. And then, when people did offer to help me practice, they would switch to dialect and carry on at the same speed. Like 'ecstatic mother' fast. There was no way to keep up with it. My translation speed was slow and it was hard to talk with people. Made me quite anxious. For a while I thought it was some kind of national joke played on the English, but I realised it's just that some people aren't good teachers. Good intentions, but not teachers. They've only ever been taught, only following their experiences. Doesn't always make for good learning. My partner Kathi started to slow down. She tried, but her youngest sister was better help.

I've cobbled together my own form of Deutsch. Even though this is Austria. There isn't really an Austrian language. They name the dialects. There is more pride, perhaps, and too many differences to embrace them as Austrian, under one name. That and the German influence is still pretty strong. I get told by my friends I

have a creative *Tirolerisch*. My cases jump and my
word choices are correct, but not the same a native
speaker would use. So, they learn to listen too, like
me, to make sense of me. Hopefully, if I can practice a
bit more it'll be easier to find work.

Martin looks from left to right, following a passing doctor.

We've started telling each other stories about our
families so I can practice. Kathi slows down when she
tells stories. I try to tell her my stories.

He looks at his watch. He has no watch.

It takes me ages to find all the right words to tell her a
story, but I always get there. She told me one about
her father's mother. Her family, her dad's family, is
part Italian and part from the Netherlands. The Dutch
part lived in Amsterdam after the Second World War.
Well, nearby the edges of the city. They had a goat
farm. They made cheese.

After the war the tourists started coming. Kathi's
grandmother didn't like the tourists it seems. As a

child, her grandmother would go across the fields following the goats with a red tin box and a silver spoon. She would follow them for the whole day, scooping up their shit pellets and collecting them in her red tin box. When she got home, she would wrap them in envelopes made from the thin pages of American Bibles that had been left behind, and sell them to the tourists as praline chocolates beside the canal bridges.

Martin's gaze follows another passing doctor.

(To self) Hebamme. *Wo is die Hebamme für Frau Martinella?*

The one I think about the most at the moment though, is a story about her great-grandfather, Bruno. He's not often a man of many words. When we go to visit, there are these big family dinners. He sits quiet at the table, drawing on something, often shaving a chock of wood or else fiddling with some gear or other in his imagination. He hums as well. Sometimes it sounds like he's accompanying his thoughts with a vaudevillian score.

If you watch him long enough, you realise everything he does makes a kind of music somehow. A percussive life.

Kathi told me one about when he was younger, when she and her sisters were younger, when the youngest, Lucia, was but a baby. Bruno still worked on his farm. He would sing to the goats. But there were some years when it wouldn't go well for cheese making. The goats wouldn't produce milk, or, one year, there was a disease that killed most of the goats.

Like most people, Bruno would go out walking to try and resolve his unease and worrisome thoughts. There were many which loomed over him; his wife, his children, their children. As he walked off the fields he would find himself at the fringes of the city of Amsterdam. He would follow the wind of the streets and look at the bicycles. Had his life started differently he would have loved to become a bicycle mechanic. The further he walked, the more bicycles he saw.

Always, everywhere, bicycles.

He stared at the chains, freckled with rust, the half deflated back tyres, the crooked handlebars and the frayed brake cables. He walked all over the city and found other bikes to stare at too. He wondered where these abandoned ones came from. On the way home, one evening, he found himself walking behind a family on bicycles clearly on holiday; the two parents ahead and a small boy lagging between them. At dinner that evening, amidst the melee of his doubts, he sat and scrubbed at a small piece of marble he had found in one of the fields.

He walked the same route for nine consecutive days. Always finding the same clumps of bicycles. And, at dusk on the tenth day, he set off into town with a bike pump and a pair of bolt cutters under his jacket. He decided on two of the more dilapidated bikes, snapped off the lock chains, pumped up the tyres and walked them home. He spent a couple days fixing them up then sold them down the Sunday market, since there was no cheese to sell.

He took Kathi and her middle sister Nicola along with

him sometimes. He let them take the abandoned children's bikes so the girls each had a bike to ride on.

His busiest time of year was autumn, as the schools reopened and the tourists fled the shortening days, leaving their debris and the remnants of joy behind. Joy? But is it joy? Perhaps that's the wrong word.

He sold enough bikes through September and October to see them through the first winter. He carried on well into the next year, earning enough to buy a new flock of goats. Life on the farm continued. And so did his side passion of acquiring and fixing up bikes. The yard was littered with chains and cassettes and wheels and random pedals.

He was dubbed St. Bruno, patron saint of the abandoned bicycle, by the family.

(To self) There is always a way.

Sound of tannoy. Martin looks up to the left of the stage and squints.

Over tannoy: Herr *Camp-bell*, Herr *Camp-bell*. (to someone beside the microphone: *Ist das richtig? Camp Bell? 'Ja,ja.'*) Herr *Camp-Bell*. Raum Oans, Raum Oans bitte.

His eyes dilate and widen at the edges. He breathes. Stands. Looks about.
Someone (next monologue) walks past him. He squeezes his thumbs discreetly. Exits left. Knocks on door and enters. Door sounds.

Martin: *(shouted off stage) Hallo Frau Hebamme.*

While the above happens, the Someone (next monologue) walks along the corridor and out the hospital door and sits at a bus stop.

Monologue 2:

Take him for a drink

Luke Dunston is sat at a bus stop. German voices can be heard in discussion and street sounds to begin with then fade. Middle stage, sat closer to the audience than first monologue.

Luke: I fucking hate being in hospitals. I can barely concentrate in them. It's like holding your breath for a week and trying to sing on Sunday. I just don't like them. Like trying to suck a bicycle through a hosepipe. And they're confusing to leave. Like today, trying to get out of the ward, I ended up in a midwife clinic! I mean, of course they're saving lives, trying to save lives. They saved my life once, but I just don't feel comfortable inside them. And now matey boy has ended up inside one. Fell out of a bloody tree didn't he. Twat. And he's the boss as well. Imagine that: a drunk arborist, swinging in a tree and cuts his own safety line with the chainsaw instead of the branch. Fell 30 feet. Lucky bastard only broke his leg. What am I supposed to do now? It's not really a one-man job.

What am I supposed to do? I haven't got enough German to start looking for another job. Shit.

Looks around at the people. A bus stops, noises of people getting on/off. Bus leaves.

I really don't like hospitals. I had to sit and wait in the café because the waiting room freaked me out. I can't handle the anguish. No one prepares you to see that, what it does to people. People pulling at their eyes and crushing their fingers. The place reeks of nervous sweat. You know, some people fart when they're nervous. Not sure why. But they do. My Great Auntie Clara used to fart when she was nervous. She used to be a bookkeeper, back in Leeds. Apparently, she'd be fine whilst doing the accounts for her brother's paint company, in her element with a pen in her hand, but whilst she was waiting to get paid, she couldn't stop farting. Big loud ones, silent stinkers. The duck walker. All kinds whilst she had to wait. Apparently she was quieter when she was younger. Then Paul got ill.

She farted a lot after that.

Luke looks down at his hands. Holds his hands together. Leans back on the bus stop. His face goes from one of remembering, sadness and then to good humour.

Towards the end, Paul was in St. James's hospital. In Leeds. He was in for observation. Taking turns, they said, as if dying was some elaborate dance. But he was pretty much bed bound. No, he was bed bound. Had to be wheeled in a chair if he wanted to go anywhere. Clara used to visit him a lot. He'd sold the paint; she'd done the books. He was tall, Paul. Tall and a great smile. Big shoulders and big ears. Ears like a football trophy handle. Giant arms.

(Beat)

Clara went to visit him one day, sometime in July. The staff nurse in the ward was fond of them. They were good fun to be around, in a simple and playful way. Witty. Clara went and sat next to Paul and they chatted on. When the nurse came round, Paul asked if she could take him for a drink. 'Of course. After his morning meds. The canteen's up on the fourth floor. We'll get you a wheelchair. Just make sure you're back by two for afternoon meds.' And they chatted on for a while until all the checks and such had been done. They gave Paul one of those hospital cardigans to keep warm. He was only wearing a gown. One of those open at the back gowns. They said thanks and set off once they got him in the wheelchair.

(Pause. Smiles at self.)

The nurse came back for his two o'clock meds. No Paul. No Clara. She rang up to the canteen on the fourth floor. No one had seen them. They put an announcement out over the hospital tannoy. Nothing. Gone. After calling the police to report a missing patient, she called Paul's son, Gary, and told him his dad was missing. She didn't say anything about Clara. Chaos ensued, as you can imagine. What didn't help was Paul was well known as a walker in the family. If something caught his imagination, or he just fancied going somewhere, he just went. Sometimes a walk could last a couple days before he returned. If he wanted to go somewhere, he'd go, but never felt like he had to tell anyone. It's his free choice, he'd always say. Didn't change much the older he got. Gary called his sister Lisa, and got them to start calling round everyone who knew their dad. Gary went round to his auntie's to see if he had turned up. No. And his auntie wasn't there either. He tried to remember where he'd gone recently, thought of the fields that opened up behind his dad's house and wondered if he could be out there again, kind of ignoring how much of an effort it would have been for Paul to get there in the first place; the stressed mind can imagine all sorts. So, Gary set off in his car towards the other side of Leeds. Along the way he called his sister again, but no sightings. Then he suddenly thought about Clara. Hadn't Clara said she was going to visit? Gary pulled over and called Clara.

(Clears his throat and prepares for an impersonation)

'Clara? Clara, can you hear me?' 'Aye, right I can love. What's the bother?' 'Dad's gone missing from the hospital! Have you heard from him? Do you know where he could be? Have you seen him?' 'Oh, aye. I can see him right now.' Gary was surprised by that bit. 'What do you mean you can see him now?' 'I mean, he's sat across from me at the table.' 'Where are you?'

'Well, it's a Friday so we're at The Fenton for a pint, before we go to the chippy. Don't worry, I asked the nurse if I could take him for a drink.' Good Catholics, fish on a Friday. Just so you know, St James's hospital is over a 2-mile walk, almost 5 kilometres, from The Fenton. Clara had pushed Paul, in his bare backed hospital gown with only a cardigan on, in the hospital wheelchair; all the way through Leeds city centre to get to the pub.

Luke pauses for thought. Looks a little less tense, less stressed than he did earlier.

Maybe someone needs a painter? I can paint walls.

Gets out phone and starts typing. Phone translator says out loud: "Ich bin ein Maler. Brauchen Sie einen Maler?" Repeats a couple times. Luke tries to say it as well

Well, why not?

A bus arrives. Next one (monologue 3) gets off and Luke gets on. Next one turns to his left.
Fade to black.

Monologue 3:

Trees

Lights come up. Tom Owens is sat on a bench in a cemetery, passing the time of day. Upset, but trying to talk normally throughout. The seat is closer to audience.

Tom: I'm glad they've got those tellies on the buses here. Tells you what stop you're approaching. Still trying to learn my way around the place. It's not so big, but big enough. And trying to learn the names for things takes a while. Sometimes they look similar, bakery and *Bäckerei*, apple and *Apfel*, but sometimes it's nothing close, potato – *Kartoffel*, cream – *Schlagobers*. *Friedhof* – cemetery.

(Pause)

It's been a strange year.

Pauses. Possibly cries then stops. Looks at the trees.

I'm not sure why I come and sit in here. I don't know. Just sat down one day when I was allowed to go out for a walk. I just saw the bench and sat down. Didn't realise I was sat in a cemetery until the second or third time I sat here. Did you know cemeteries are one of the few public spaces where it's free to sit down and you're not surrounded by demands to consume anything?

(Looks around) It's calm here. And I like the trees. Sometimes I see the fruit emerge, grow and ripen. One thing I never understood, why not have more fruit trees in public spaces? We could all eat then, no?

Looks at the trees. Bird song.

I met a man who likes trees last week. A couple months ago I managed to get a job at a community centre. Reception duties, bit of cleaning. Helping out. They could only give me a 10 hour a week contract, but it means I can get health insurance.

(Pause) I was talking to the lady who organises the event programme one day, and she said that a festival

was happening in Vienna. The community centre had been invited to send someone to be part of a day-long international conference, to give a presentation about communal spaces. I asked who was going and she said they hadn't decided. I asked if it would be in English or German. She reckoned English because she doubted everyone there would speak all the languages. English is still a kind of default language. So, I offered. I told her I was alright at talking in front of people. She spoke to the rest of the team and they said it was fine with them. So I asked what the presentation was about. Financing common spaces. Finance. She said I could talk to the people in the team who were more responsible for that side of things. I just had to explain how the centre's finances worked. Not my own.

(Pause) I got in contact with the people at the festival and told them who I was. They got me a train ticket and said they'd put me up in a hotel for the couple of nights I was there. Fine by me. When I told my partner, she was proud of me. She laughed when I told her I had to talk about finance. When we had first met, I had to pay for the drinks with a sock full of pennies,

but that was then. Now I was going to Vienna to talk about Finance.

Vienna is kind of split by the river Danube. The bit that most people see, the old part and the shops and stuff, is on one side. The hotel I was staying at was on the other. Really interesting place. It had once been an old people's home, but had been closed down. A community group got inside and set up a soup kitchen. Not sure how, but then they put together the plan to turn it into a hotel. The city agreed and they ran it as a community and integration project. The place is part run by people who have arrived from all over the world. Austria's a pretty hard country to be an outsider in, so it's massive for the people who work there. Inside it's so comfortable and clean, a bit makeshift and DIY, but welcoming.

The first night, I kept to myself. I saw some people who I guessed were also in for the conference, but somehow, I didn't want to talk to them. Wanted to be alone, but not alone, but alone. It was the first time I'd be away from my partner for a long time. It felt wrong. But she called to check in on me later that night and we talked about it.

I read over my notes for the presentation before bed. Then slept a bit.

I had my breakfast, but still couldn't bring myself to talk to anyone in the café. I got on the wrong train to the venue for the conference, but arrived on time. I was speaking in the last round of the day. The other talks were interesting. About the legal and other ways to occupy buildings for community projects. Incredible how many countries really seem to be run by people who just don't give a fuck about communities for people, outside giving them places to buy stuff. How often do you really find a place where you can just be? In a common space? Where chance meetings can really happen?

I mean, places that aren't just cemeteries.

They took a break before my round, but I went and sat in my seat at the front and waited there. I didn't have the history the other people had to share. I was new to all this. For a couple minutes I felt really out of place and had to concentrate on breathing slower. But it was fine. I stuck to my notes, didn't go off on any tangents. Explained in a simple way, no academic terms or anything. Answered a few questions in the Q and A. By the end I felt comfortable. After doing the presentation I felt like I could talk with everyone and listen better, so I joined in a bit. The organisers took us all out for dinner. Somehow, by the time the falafel durum was before me, I'd found some of my talkative soul and held forth a bit at the table. It was great. A little moment of feeling alive again.

I agreed to share breakfast with one of the other speakers, a lady from Belgrade. I'm always an early riser and she had to catch a plane home. I went down first and said I'd call at 7 if she wasn't there.

As part of the festival, we got offered breakfast as well. But the amount they paid was only for the slice of cheese and bread one, so I looked at the menu and decided pay the difference and try the Arabic breakfast.

(Pauses. Looks at the trees) I don't know about you,

but have you ever seen something that's been made with love? It has this kind of aura about it. You can see the care and affection that was part of it. It kind of glows a bit. I almost couldn't eat it. Milk rice with pomegranate seeds, goat's cheese, warm fresh rolls, falafel and some kind of tomato salad. It was so colourful. Like looking at some kind of Islamic mosaic. I don't know what came over me, but I didn't know how to eat it. I stood up and walked through the café, I found the kitchen door and I stepped inside. It was really loud; the pot wash was beside the door and it was on. I looked around and could only see one person by the cooker. I walked up to him and, in my best attempt at German, said hello. He was surprised. He turned around. I think we were both nervous, but I was possessed. I felt so full of urgency and grief and German verb structures, and panic; all sloshing around in my head. But I asked him what the most beautiful word he knew was.

He didn't understand. He started to look around the kitchen a bit anxious. I repeated my question. I started to feel anxious as well. Fuck. What if he thinks I'm an immigration officer or something? I asked again, and

from behind me came a voice in Nigerian English.
'Excuse me, sir, this is the kitchen. This is not for you.'
'But I need to know, is he the cook?' 'Yes, this
morning, but sir…" 'Then ask him, please, what is the
most beautiful word he knows?'

I was stuck in between these two men. The first one
staring at the waiter, waiting, expecting and hoping for
an easy end. The waiter spoke to him in a gentle
language, like poetry pooled in the eddy of a calm
river that drifted over me at its own pace. The chef
looked at me, then at the waiter. Then spoke to the
waiter, but looked at me.

'He said, trees.' 'Ask him why? Why trees?' And he
did. By now I was almost crying. I could feel my eyes
filling up. I watched the chef's face as he answered this
ridiculous question. I stepped a little to the side and
looked at the waiter as he began to answer. I was
almost side by side with the chef.

'He said, trees. Trees is his most beautiful word. When
he was a child and lived at his home in a compound
with his family, they had a tree, a tall tree in the

middle of the compound. He used to dream of being a bird. In his bird dream he would lay enough eggs for his sisters to eat, then go and sit on the branch to see over the walls of the compound and watch out for signs of trouble, to keep his sisters safe.'

I turned the chef and told him, 'With this breakfast you have given me trees.' The waiter translated and the chef seemed to understand and smiled at me. I left the kitchen. Maybe this sounds ridiculous to you. I don't know. I think I was still crying when the lady from Serbia sat down beside me.

(Pauses. Looks at the trees.) You know, sometimes I think it's weird sitting here – with all this madness and selfishness going on around me. But I need this. There's so little I can do here. I don't think it's too much, just to sit and look at the trees for a while.

Birdsong. Fade to black.

Intermission for tongues

I wonder how your tongue moves as you sing, as you dream. I wonder how your mouth shapes the hushed, murmured words in your sleep. How does your throat resonate as you sing, as you sigh? Are you sympathetic to the original sound? Are you familiar with the oscillator?

How fresh is the air in your larynx? Can you mimic the aria of a clarinet? Can you bow it like a cello? Can you hum like a chanting monk? Can you call like a stonecutter finch on the mountainside?

I wonder how your vocal cords shiver as you share your thoughts, as you laugh, as you express a single note out into the world around you, as you cry out in the cascade of bliss.

I wonder what languages you speak. What do you think a language is anyway?

What symbols can you whisper?

I wonder if you've found your voice.

I wonder.

Were you ever taught to seek it?

Do you have a favourite word to sing?

What would you say into the echo chamber? What would you call into the abyss?

What would you shout from the top of the hill? From the depths of the valley?

What word do you long to hear?

I wonder.

Resume

11   Focaccia for you and sweeping

I enjoy the search for something to share with you, to satisfy our hunger. I am beyond concern for time. I'm sure I will arrive at the station for my train. The train. It's not my train. As if I could afford a train. If I could I probably would have better shoes than these.

But I won't bore you with time. I hand you something to eat

—

Thank you for waiting. Here's a focaccia for you. Someone recommended this place over there. Word of mouth sounds so much more appetising to me, and my stomach.

Thank you for being patient. We could move somewhere else if you want to?

And did the play encourage any thoughts in you?

—

I wish I could talk with you.

—

What did it remind me of? First thing it brought to my mind was my love of sweeping.

I have been a cleaner many times in my life. My first job as a teenager. And I enjoyed sweeping. I enjoyed finding a rhythm for each motion. I enjoyed the repetitive nature of the actions I would make. It made me feel comfortable, expansive and able to contemplate my thoughts, my selves. It made me sing. I would try to create games, games of distraction, funny situations, scenarios inspired by sweeping. That's one place where I learnt to enjoy my own sense of humour.

We were in a team of cleaners. If anyone started acting a dick, or not being responsible, we'd start hiding their equipment until they realised that they had to settle down and communicate with the rest of us. Or we would sing about the parts of that person that we enjoyed, that we wanted them to remember. Just in case they had forgotten themselves.

I remember sweeping up in the auditorium of a theatre.

I liked that. Being inside with only the ghost light on, thinking my thoughts. Sweeping up the debris, the spectre of catharsis, the echoes of wishes and longings, the responses to the evenings performance that resonate until all the energy dissipates and spills out of the open doors. Airing out the room. I remember sweeping up in the corridors of a school, surrounded by the carnival of youthful smells and dreams. I remember sweeping the rooms of a library after the revelry of a book fair. I, I think I've found it. The favourite memory I have of sweeping. No. How can there be a singular favourite. Forget that. The notion of living by comparison is also a nuisance. Excuse me. One memory I have is of a time in Catalonia.

I went to Barcelona. It was April of 2011. I arrived as the country was in the midst of an uprising. I got lost in the city centre. I found myself in a big public square, surrounded by tents and chanting, people of all ages and, and they would gather in the evenings. They would form a giant mass of people in the square that would spill over into the streets. I saw a photograph, an ariel photograph of it in a paper, some 20,000 people all together. Or was it more? I forget. But I remember being welcome there. They discussed their desires and needs. I lost the place where I was supposed to sleep, caught up in the moment of it all. I told someone. And I was invited to sleep in the square with everyone else. I remember, in the mornings, there would be a list of things that needed to be sourced and jobs that needed doing. I didn't read Spanish, still can't. But I asked someone and they showed me in a kind of pantomime. Not long after I was laughing and sweeping up the Plaça de Catalunya in the warmth of the April morning sun. I enjoyed that.

But I digress.

12   *To myself*

I lean back and feel the chair ribs push up against me. There is a murmur from elsewhere. Orders pour into the waiter's ears. You turn, your eyes searching for the street. The passing squall influences the light of the sky. The swirling shadows draw the attention of the day's spectators. A pebble nicks the glass. A thread of lightning. A jet of steam from the coffee machine. The call of the kitchen porter's bell. The boom and report of the thunder. If all we are witnessing is the discharge of clouds, why does it have two words? Have you ever considered that clouds are both some of the loudest and quietest participants of life here on earth?

You return from your seeking and our eyes find one another. We exhale and, perhaps, we enter the trance of the liminal. Again.

We indulge in the silence together. It is the space for existence to breathe, the ocean between individuals that does not isolate, but connects them. There is where we live now. With the urgency of inquisitive bliss. Here, here in this realm. It is a chamber with walls as fine as falling water, adorned with pulsing orbs of aureolin, vermillion, emerald and sapphire, patterns of light erupt and die, exciting the colours so they bleed; as the spirits of ours and the cities ancestors push their fingers through the veil to draw their messages on the veneer of the moment. That there is already a word for what we are striving for, living for. Not just being within the absence of something else. Not just legitimising that other which we seek not to be.

But that is too far. To see that one word, if we said it enough, may birth other words. Other places we could act in, inhabit. That a single word, satyagraha, *an invocation. Not just an absence. The poetry of existence, the interweave of it all. The joyful side of limerence. Of being.*

Our gaze could hold each other within this dance, interlinking thoughts' fingers in a delicate embrace. It is supportive. Dialogue of the enchanted. Elements of intercourse. Nourishing the canny weave of our species. The sheer, luminous joy of time with a stranger. This is restorative. Just is.

We are here until we exhale, until the moment dies. Until we are undone.

We are here until we begin again. We are. We stand to leave together.

–

I stand up to leave.

13   Perhaps

On the threshold of the street my thoughts wander before I take my first step. I must remember the time my train leaves, but I don't want such a responsibility. I check the onward ticket in my pocket, printed on that odd soft card. I still have a little longer here.

Outside we see the rains reappear. The rain turns to hail. We marvel at it. We might be silent. The world outside is not.

–

That hail. Perhaps we'll eat here, under the awning. If it slowed down it would look like pollen. Have you ever seen a pollen blizzard?

I saw one, once. I was cleaning up at a works yard, somewhere on the river Avon. I had my back to the water, staring at the grooves in the floor. Sweeping my brush this way and that. Then, I remember seeing a tuft of pollen come drifting over my shoulder. The colour of sorbet and horse-hair as it drifted in and out of the sunlight, before showing a dull white as it fell in my shadow. Slow and calm, I turned around and found myself watching a whirling, flourishing blizzard of pollen. The world around me was all a-dance, everywhere I looked. Shimmering light, soft and inspired by the will of the wind.

The will of the wind.

Aye. By the will of the wind. I think I fetched myself a stool and sat down to watch it for a while. Yes, to take it in.

\-

We perch on the step, betwixt two worlds. Maybe we become patient, simultaneously; deciding without words.

\-

Dante piange! Siate pazienti. Il cambiamento è in arrivo.

\-

We wait. Perhaps we eat the focaccia.

14   *Jellyfish. Chess. Ljubljana. Luka.*

And, as always, it changes. The rain eases and ceases to fall.

We finish our breads, revived. I exhale and step out upon the wet cobbles, hoping you'll join me, both of us wearing our masks of mischief and levity, striding across the shoulders of the city's slumbering titans. Our feet will not stay warm or dry for long as we follow the course of the flooding waters. It guides, we trust, towards Piazza Bellini. But we are in no rush. We accompany the branches and tributaries, meandering through the arteries of the San Lorenzo district. Whether by intuition or by circumstance, at some junctions we agree to travel upstream.

The smooth, wet surfaces dishevel our myths of gravity; our centres of orientation. We slow down. We can always choose to. We respect the environment beneath our feet, becoming lithe and liquescent; lest we desire to make fools of ourselves. Time is but a narcissist's imitation of circadian rhythms. It can be ignored at will. The rain helps us remember many truths.

As we amble, I tuck my hands into my trouser pockets.

My fingers encounter something soft and fine. With a delicate motion I tuck it between my first and middle finger. I pull it out and hold it before us. It is a small feather, no bigger than my thumb. As I turn it over, I cast about in my memories for where it may have come from. I hear an eerie song across a bay. I taste salt on my lips. The vision of women wading into the sea wearing only woven skirts, their bare breasts taunting the wind. I open my mouth and the peculiar voice of a black-throated loon pours free. It's from near the Strunjan peninsula, I think to myself.

—

Do you know where Slovenia is? Did you ever hear about the jellyfish in Ljubljana? I reckon this might last as long as our path to Café Araba. Here, you hold this feather as we find our way.

—

In 1945 someone said the phrase 'never again'. Some other people also said it. Then when t-shirts became popular, they put it on them so it might never again be forgotten. They also put it on stickers, teacups, door mats, history exam papers, brick walls and I believe, at some point, it was even etched with a knife onto the passenger side door of John Major's car. So many people said it, saw it and wrote this phrase down that towards the end of the 20th century it really meant nothing at all. So, people forgot and were dragged back to war; wars that they're still fighting now.

In order to get away from the news of all the fighting and ball of confusion that life now resembles, I left the city I was living in and travelled over land to Ljubljana to visit a friend. My friend's name is Petra. If you translate her name into English then she's really called *Stone Fox*. But, for other reasons I call her Pea. She was studying for a Masters in translation at that moment. Despite being in a class deciphering Japanese, she had time to send me a message, telling me to go in search of a café called *Jellyfish*, and that she'd find me once she was finished.

The *Jellyfish*, fortunately for me, is quite close to the main campus building. Well, the main building for Architecture. I walked across the *Sent Jakobski Most* and into the *Tivoli Park*, then found it tucked away in one of the corners. As soon as I had asked someone passing by, they smiled and directed me there.

It's not really, legally speaking, a café, or a bar. It's more of a shack; improvised. Most of the tables have chessboards drawn on them. Tufts of grass blanket the feet and dandelion stems crawl up the legs. They were all covered over with wicker and simple wooden chairs when I found it. The bushes around the tables showed the heads of the rhododendrons choosing what colour to bloom. The golden ash trees shivered in the wind; pairs of old leather shoes were laced together and hanging from the lower branches. There were no flags, no trinkets, no rabbit's tooth charms or decorations hanging about. There were tin cans though, with the labels peeled off and polish rubbed round the lip, full of shoe shine brushes, which leant a bitter tang to the air. No television, no wifi. Besides the tables and a glass-doored cabinet full of schnapps glasses, there was a rickety old oak bookshelf with a radio perched on top. Socks filled with sets of chess pieces hung on nails down its side. On the middle shelf sat a couple shoe boxes with spare pieces, all washed up from elsewhere, from other lives.

I turned over a chair and sat down. As I did a light came on and cleared out the darkness of the kitchen. In the glow it resembled a kebab shop mixed with a bakery, that someone had tried to stuff into a lean-to shed, only most of the walls were missing.

The light caught my attention as it flickered and, like a medieval travelling theatre wagon, the hotplates opened up and hummed, an old upright piano was wheeled out of the gangway. The rotisseries spun and the cabinets filled up with an assortment of hands lining up the giant rolled bureks. I watched as one of the men dragged the piano out beside the tables and teased a couple of notes from the keys.

One of the men behind the counter looked up and we saw one another. To my left appeared one of the other men, like a Bosnian genie or fakir with, to my surprise, a plate and a glass of schnapps in his hand.

"Plum," he said

"Plum what?"

"Burek."

"Plum burek?" I asked confused.

He shook his head once, put down the burek and put down the glass.

"Plum," he wiggled the little finger on his left hand that was wrapped around the glass, "Burek, cheese," he wiggled the other little finger and grinned.

"I see."

"No, I see. You eat."

A row of lanterns crackled into life over our heads.

"*Shaskabiti!*" yelled someone in the kitchen.

"Thanks," I picked up the glass and caught the scent of spirits, "but I don't drink alcohol," I told him.

"That's ok," he plucked the glass from my grasp between thumb and forefinger, holding it up to one of the lanterns, "and I don't speak English," he said in a friendly manner.

With a childish grin spreading over his cheeks, he drained the glass and headed back to the kitchen. I bit into the burek and found the pastry soft, warm, delicious.

I received another message from Pea. She was on her way.

I looked about the bushes, seeing the flickering lights of passing cars weave between them like fireflies. On the edge of the park, the city flags swung drunk in the wind. People, humans of all variety, sifted about the dusky streets for a place to rest or undress stress in one way or another.

More bulbs flickered overhead. The radio was turned on and the dial cocked to a position that channelled a scronky jazz record with someone singing over the top; alternating between the wails of a junior muezzin and the beatitude of an imam.

A young couple came by and bought some burek to carry away. An older man, in a fine tailored suit and frayed shoes, sat on a stumpy wicker chair at another table waiting to be seen. The staff, as such, carried on turning flour, puckering up doughs and teasing spinach in a jet-black skillet pan as it simmered in its juices, and chopped wild chilis dancing in the oil. One moved aside to fill an ornate, turquoise samovar with mint tea, the greenish liquid plumped up with clotted leaves and the berries from a juniper tree.

I went up to the bookshelf looking for something to turn over before Pea arrived. Most of the spines were in Slovene, German or an array of languages I had no names for. The only book I found that had been translated into English was *The Walnut Mansion by Miljenko Jergovic*. As I sat down, I found a glass of tea waiting for me. A small mountain of sugar stood on the saucer alongside a spoon the shape of a fallen carob fruit. I watched the sugar sink through the tea as I stirred and pulled open the book cover.

"I hate it when that happens," Pea sat down beside me. "When you just get yourself ready to begin a book and someone, or something else, arrives to cut you off, as if there weren't enough interruptions these days."

It had been four years since we had seen one another, but some people have a canny knack of ignoring, or being outside of time; she is one of them.

"Don't ask about my class, it was slow and figurative."

"Do you want something to eat?"

"It'll be ready soon."

"Have you also turned clairvoyant since we last met?"

"No, I just eat here a lot. It's more comfortable than being canned inside the library like a herring."

A waiter appeared at both of her shoulders. A plate of potato burek topped with sesame seeds and a pot of tea was put down before her. She stood and shook hands with both of the men. The three of them discussed something in a makeshift language, a mix of Bosnian and Slovene; the lilt and drift of the vowels ebbing away from me and banking up on the grass like pollen fleece. They left, parting with a duet of *'Shaskabiti'* and Petra sat down again.

"Popular here?"

"Yes, makes a welcome change from the university lot and home."

"What does this word mean? *Shaskabiti?*"

"It comes from a story, written down by a wandering Slovene, one who sometimes eats here. I'll tell you another time. Where are you staying tonight?" she asked.

"At a hostel, just down the way."

"I've been dreaming of living there for years."

"At the hostel?"

"No, just down the way."

"Still a charming way with words."

"For now, but as soon as this semester is finished, I'm leaving, again. Not sure where, maybe even to Peru, but perhaps anywhere I can find work."

"I'll let you know if I hear of anything over our way."

We fell into the silence of eating and drinking. A young lady sat at the piano and played chords along with the radio. Pea turned over the burek and tucked in. I sipped at my tea, sifting out the leaves and berries with my teeth. She watched me for a while as I watched the customers as they filled the tables. Everyone was attended to as if they were family.

"Do you have any idea how they got here?" Pea asked.

"Who?"

"The guys running the place."

"No. Do you?"

"Yes. Did you ever hear the story about the only jellyfish ever found in Ljubljana?"

"No. How would it have got it here from the sea?"

"Well, it didn't swim from Slovenia's tiny concession of a coastline, but it did come from there."

She finished eating the piece of burek in her hand, then stroked a napkin with her greasy fingers.

"There is a saying," she began, "'*Bosnians never lie*'. I don't know how true it is, but it's true enough for this history. See those three over there behind the counter? Yes, they started this place back in the 90s and look, just above the fridge, in the frame, that's a photo of Luka, well everyone here calls him 'cousin Luka'. He was here when they started, but he left. He's the one who this place is named after, and it has nothing to do with being spineless.

"The three brothers – Antonijo, Bepo, Marko;" she gestured to the men behind the counter, "and their cousin Luka once lived in Bosnia Herzegovina, near Visegrad, to the east of Sarajevo. I heard from someone else that they'd really been in Srebrenica, but I heard different from the brothers and I never really wanted to challenge them on it. Some points are too fine to debate," she paused to pour her tea.

"The brothers had no-one except themselves, but cousin Luka had a wife and new born child. The infant was so young that Luka and his wife Dijana didn't even have time to name her before they had to flee from Milošević's soldiers." She blew the steam from the top of the cup and took a sip.

"Luka and his wife agreed to meet in Jajce and head to Slovenia," Pea continued. "The meeting point was her uncle's house. Cousin Luka couldn't stand her uncle. He was a drunk, all his teeth rotten out from home-made brandy. When Luka complained about her choice, she pointed out it was the furthest point from Visegrad that they'd been to together. She didn't know where else to suggest. They had only been there once, shortly after their wedding to share a meal with that part of her family. Cousin Luka accepted."

She wrapped both hands around the cup and looked at me for a moment. Her fingers were illuminated by a rouge lantern above the table and by a yellow glow from another set of lights, that made her hair shine golden in the darkness drawing in. She put down the cup.

"The next day they said goodbye was one of the worst days of their relationship for sure."

"But why did they split up?"

"Milošević's soldiers were targeting men, boys; as long as they were Muslim and male they were to be treated to slaughter. War forces us into the tragedy of circumstance. The women had more of a chance. Luka kissed his wife and daughter and began to run into the forest.

"He and the brothers didn't stop until they saw the waterfall in Jajce. For the whole journey, cousin Luka held onto the knowledge that his wife would be following only a day behind with a group of seven other women. It sustained him on the days they found no food or shelter, when they heard violence surrounding them. The uncle wasn't at the house when they found it. They sorted through the preserves and food supplies left in the cellar, leaving the gum-rotting brandy well alone, but saving a portion of the breads, cheeses, oils and plum jam for his wife's group."

She took up her tea cup again and drank.

"They waited for over two months before the brothers told Luka they ought to keep moving," said Pea.

"Fuck." I didn't know what else to say.

"They stayed for one more night, but by sunrise she still wasn't there. The light of the sun fell, heavy inside each of his tears as they walked north. Outside a house, near the Croatian border, cousin Luka saw the familiar label of his uncle's brandy on a crate beside the door. Some odd curiosity rose up in him. He went and knocked on the door. An old, creased lady came to the door and stood behind the shutter. He asked how much for a bottle of brandy and for a reply she spat on the floor and shouted that if she ever found the bastard who made it, she would cut out his eyes and stuff them up his arse because it had rotted all her teeth down the stubbly stumps."

"Grim."

"Booze. But he also asked if he could use her phone. For a moment she hesitated, uncertainty flashing in her steel grey eyes before she permitted him. He dialled the number for his uncle's house. The old lady carried on cursing the man, unaware of the connection, whilst the brothers cleaned their shoes on the grass in her front garden. He stared after them, until he heard a whispering voice replace the dial tone. *'Dijana?'* he whispered back. *'Yes, Luka'* was all he heard. *'I'm coming for you, I'm at the Croatian border. Stay there.'* He kissed the phone and the hands of the old lady. She slapped him away. He explained to the brothers. They agreed to head north and wished him well. He didn't stop walking for a day and a half. As he reached the front door he collapsed and slumped onto the tatty wooden porch. Dijana opened up and kissed his cheeks before dragging him inside.

"A couple days later, I think he said it was a Wednesday, the pair set out for Ljubljana."

"But where was their daughter?" I asked.

"Sadly, she died on the way. Too young and too delicate."

"Fuck, that's terrible."

"I didn't hear it from Luka. Bepo told me that Dijana said she just couldn't breathe anymore. No matter what the women tried, the child just slowly stopped breathing."

I folded my arms around my ribs. I don't know why I do it. I do it unconsciously. I held myself and looked around at the other people. Someone had turned the radio down. The young woman at the piano was singing in Cameroonian French, lisping a little, but letting her voice fill the evening twilight. The old man, in the pinstripe suit, was looking at a polaroid photograph. He slid it back into his breast pocket. I watched him, as he observed everyone else. He raised his hand to order. I looked at Pea.

"But where did they head to when they left Jajce?"

"They came here, to Slovenia, to Ljubljana."

"But, why Ljubljana?"

"The Slovenes were considered more welcoming. It was further from Serbia than Croatia and the soil was more fertile. When they arrived, it was only good chance and shoes that brought him and the brothers back together. This was the 90s, before mobile phones were considered so necessary. Remember then? Anyway, cousin Luka followed a hunch and headed for the main bus station." She stopped rolling the cup between her hands and put it down again.

"Why shoes and the bus station?" I asked.

"It was part of a peculiar, shared sibling rivalry. Each of them adored fashionable shoes. Or at least adored them enough to try and 'get one up' on each other. So, they'd set up a little shoe shine bench at the bus station to make money for food."

"But, why the bus station?"

"Train stations have more police, less old people and too many trainers, not shoes that need shining. So, there he found them; scrubbing away, dusting ankles and licking leather with cloths made from torn off shirt-cuffs. That night they had a reunion party in the corner of a park where the three brothers slept. They were still a little way off from affording a room. Cousin Luka and Dijana joined them and shared a camping bed they had found discarded in an alley.

"The brothers were also busy hatching plans aplenty in their chatter, but it was only the idea of a café that caught cousin Luka's attention. It was the only one that made sense. A local church took pity on Bepo and Marko and lent them a coffee urn. Antonijo borrowed a few cups and spoons from here and there and with the shoe shine savings they bought the coffee. It took a while, but they managed to attract the attention of the students. Fortunately, it paid off. After a couple months they fashioned an oven from parts and scraps they haggled out of a junkyard and were able to cook burek. More students came. The local authorities turned a blind eye. What is the State to gain from stopping a suffering man's entrepreneurship? It would have cost them more in benefits and housing, so they were allowed to carry on. They managed to pay for a two-room apartment near, but not too near, the park just in time for autumn.

"By the time the siege had finished and Sarajevo had become a word for international guilt, much like Gaza is nowadays, the five of them had been able to buy a couple of old cooking units, hot plates, a fridge, a gas supply, sheet metal for a roof and an old, three-door Peugeot."

I looked over her shoulder at the kitchen space.

"Pretty much how it looks now," she said, noticing where my eyes had strayed. "But, in 1997, cousin Luka arrived to work a shift and found the brothers huddled in conference. If rumours were right, one of the Chetnik generals had also wound up in Ljubljana. He'd been seen drunk and singing down the alleys, near the illegal house bars around *Cesta v Mestni log*. Apparently, one of the house bars was Serbian only and he was a regular.

"That night, not telling Dijana, cousin Luka went out in search of the alleys to see if it was true."

"But, how did they know what he looked like?"

"Someone had been handing around an article with a photo of him standing proud and smoking outside a hospital. Under the photo was his name and rank in the army and that he'd survived some kind of surgery and was ready for action.

"Cousin Luka had the brothers' copy of the paper. If it was really him then he would have had a role in the death of their child and their shared grief. He wanted to know if it was true or not.

"Wandering around the alleys he found one littered with so much broken glass it looked like a carpet of stars under the streetlights. Halfway down the alley, a door swung open and he ducked closer to the wall. He heard the distant, guttural shouts of a drunk Serb. He stood and watched the drunk wander out the top end of the alley. He walked up and found a shadow to hide in near the door. Soon enough, people started leaving and one of them was the General in the picture; all lit up with the malicious and ignorant grin of the inebriated.

"Cousin Luka waited until the alley was silent again before he left, crying as he walked home to Dijana. At the apartment he found her asleep in the living room, her hair draped over the arm of the sofa and her feet tucked under the cushions. He woke her gently. *'I have seen a horrible thing my love, I need to go to the sea to wash my eyes.'* She held his cheek and kissed his forehead, nodding as she lay her head on the pillow once more.

"He took the car and drove straight to the town of Piran, near the salt flats of Strunjan. He left his car near the harbour and sat beside the Adriatic. It didn't take long to start, but he cried for a long time. As the sun rose that morning he was still going. An Italian fisherman from Trieste, who had stayed the night at a lover's house in town, overheard him and sat beside him. As cousin Luka began to answer his questions, the fisherman realised it wouldn't be a short answer. He picked up cousin Luka and invited him to continue on his boat. They set off across the Gulf of Trieste at a slow pace. The fisherman offered Luka a beer and opened one for himself.

'And what would you do to that man,' asked the fisherman.

'I thought about killing him, but when I looked at myself, it's not in me, and that twists me even more!'

'What if you had help?' and he cocked his fingers like a pistol.

'I don't think I could ever do it.'

'You know, *they* can kill.'

'What?'

'Jellyfish.'

Bobbing alongside the boat, rubbing their greasy, gelatinous heads on the hull, was a field of jellyfish, stuck to the surface and glowing like an open face of charoite in the morning sun.

'Them?'

'Yeah, yes, of course. There are a couple different types here. I can't remember if both might help or just the purple ones.'

'What purple one?'

'Pelagia noctiluca. Some call it 'the mauve stinger', others 'the purple people eater'.'

'But could it really kill someone?'

'I heard so, in some cases, it might give a big enough sting to an old man. And, if not, he'll suffer for the rest of his little while.'

"Well, that's a kind of approximation of the conversation. Who knows what language they spoke in. But they understood one another. So, the two of them set about catching one of each type of a jellyfish. The blue and white cool box, that looked after the fisherman's beer, was emptied and used to preserve them. They shared one more bottle and headed back to Piran.

"The fisherman gave cousin Luka a pair of thick, leather gloves to protect himself from the poison. He wedged the cool-box in the footwell on the passenger side of his car and headed back to Ljubljana through the waning afternoon.

"He didn't go home. He didn't go in search of the brothers or go past the café. Instead, he made his way to that district in the heart of Ljubljana and found somewhere to park the car near the alleyway. He waited out the hours. Drunks are creatures of habit, or so some say, and I'd be tempted to agree. After the light of the day had ebbed and been tucked away, he spotted the general. Cousin Luka put on the gloves and got out of the car to follow, at a distance, the already lumbering figure of the general. Once inside the mouth of the glass-glittering alley, cousin Luka put down the cool box and picked out a jellyfish. He screamed, as loud as his nerves would allow, and cried out *'Shaskabiti!'* and in the moment the general spun around, he threw the slobbery mass straight into his face and ran. The last thing cousin Luka saw was the general falling and writhing on the broken glass.

"Unfortunately, not long after cousin Luka fled, the general got up from the glassy street, cutting his hands and forearms as he did so. He propped himself up against the wall, the tangy bitter taste of sea salt and algae on his lips. The remains of the barrel jellyfish shivered on the street beside him.

"In his trained, defensive nature he looked about the alley, seeking his attacker, but found no-one. As he stood up, he saw only the cool-box by the mouth of the alley. He took a cursory look inside and, at the bottom corner below the ice he saw a brown glass bottle, still closed and undisturbed."

She leant back on her chair. I felt myself being pulled towards her, as if we were connected by a line of thread. She stretched out her arms. She clenched and released her fists then poured both of us the last of her tea.

"The article in the paper the following week was only an inch and near the back," she continued, "but the post mortem declared death brought on by anaphylactic shock caused by a jellyfish sting. The poison from the purple people eater that had still been in the cool box must have got straight into his blood and to his heart."

The lanterns bobbed in the wind and the loose lengths of wire that wound down to the plug gathered and unfurled. A few more customers sat and ate. The older man, in his fine tailored suit and frayed shoes, had left. The lady still sat at the piano, but was playing along with the radio again. People wiped grease from their cheeks and others folded the tea inside their glasses with sugary spoons. The traffic beyond the tree-line wrapped the inner city in an aria of evening.

One of the brothers was moving around the guests, tucking tufts of paper into the pockets of his woollen waistcoat.

"More tea?" he asked as he picked up Pea's plate.

"Yes, please," she replied

"*Shaskabiti*," and with a graceful turn he headed, once more, to the samovar.

—

The silence of the listener encompasses the symphony of the street, life is never truly silent. Our desire for it to be so is perhaps just our lack of calm, the absence of being content.

Perhaps we long for our stories to fill that gap or else change the music of life. Perhaps.

—

That reminds me, what time is my train? Of course, you don't know. I'm supposed to remember that.

Intermission for eyes

I wonder how your emotions move you. How they tantalize and tense the fibres of your body. How they share your intrigue. I wonder what inspires the lightness in your soul.

We allow our eyes to find each other. Maybe there are nuances. Maybe we have different choices, perhaps our desires, or actions, are imperfect. But perhaps there is space for that also. Perhaps. We are by nature imperfect. Perfection is only another idea that will fail. It will be undressed and it will expire. It will come to pass. We can help that happen. If we choose to.

I breathe out.

I look into your eyes again and the will to move escapes me. I am captured, transfixed.

I am sure I watched them change colour, just now, from grey to lucid blue. Encircling your iris is a pulsing gold, as if I were watching the moon eclipse the sun. Your eyes are glowing. Did you know that?

I wonder, what you have seen in this life of yours. What do you long to see?

I wonder, what or who you have beheld, discovered, augured with those eyes.

Why do we ask about where our eyes have come from?

I wonder, how do your eyes dance while you dream?

What do you foresee?

What has hindsight taught you?

Is it through our eyes we also express our bravery? It is our eyes that make us responsible, I believe.

Through our eyes we are influenced by the world. What if, through our eyes, we remembered we could influence the world? What if we remembered our eyes are the confluence between the world and ourselves?

Résumé

15   Juggling birds of sand

There are days when I wake up and I want only one thing: to witness the beauty that persists despite all the greed. My gaze can find it without me having to search for it. The falling leaf. The people moving about their lives. The play of light through the air. People emerging from doorways. The small gestures.

Ah. I am beginning to love this street. Did I tell you yet? Did I tell you? Look, here is a man playing a kora. Listen to him. Stop what you're doing and listen a while.

–

We stop to listen, standing huddled in a doorway.

–

Now, really. That's wonderful. See their faces? See how they change a little as it reaches them. Isn't it marvellous? Imagine if they could also slow down a little bit more. A little less preoccupied. A little less tense. A little more themselves.

A little more cared for. A little more supported.

–

As we listen to the kora player a thread of lightning touches down somewhere nearby in the city. All the street lamps, restaurant lights, bedside bulbs flicker and disappear in a single pulse.

–

See, none of this is inevitable, no singular future fuelled by electricity. It's all just as fragile as everything else.

Come, let us walk in the dawn of twilight until they figure themselves out. Ah, I remember what it means, that word: *Shaskabiti*.

There was a trombone player, Peter Kralj, who played for the Slovene 6 Balkan Ska Orkestra. He joined the band when he was only 14. The schools had all dismissed him as an incorrigible teenager, an utterly hopeless case. It was only the music teachers that had defended him during the expulsion panels. Peter had a way of breathing through brass that was unique. But no matter how they pleaded, he was always put out.

The last teacher to stand in his corner hung around after the meeting was adjourned. He stopped Peter and his mother before they got to their car. The teacher had a friend, a band leader called Cecil. He wanted to introduce Peter to him, with the hope of turning Peter into a musician instead of leaving him at the mercy of circumstance. He had already started stealing alcohol from the corner shops and drinking in the park.

The mother consented and went along to the rehearsal rooms. The introduction turned into an audition turned into an invitation to join the band.

Wiley and wiry limbed, he would dance about the bars where the band performed. Some nights, if he drank too much, he would whoop and blow, but also harass the audience with such furore that in some places he'd end the night with a black eye, a bent slide and a buckled bell. He would fight back with the strength of an older man; fierce, but with the peculiar innocence of the inebriated child he still was. To him, it was all a game. Seized with the excitement of the music he would bounce, brawl and revel with everyone and everything in his way. Even, at times, with the band.

"You're good, but not untouchable! You're no king, Peter Kralj," the band leader warned him on the night before his 23rd birthday. They were on tour in Bosnia, heading for Sarajevo. Peter was sat down and given an ultimatum, somewhere between Banja Luka and Jajce. "Dance with them, rile them up, but stop fighting with them or we'll dump you in the Miljacka and leave you there with the plastic fishes."

Peter was still by far the youngest in the Orkestra. He had a lot of catching up to do, in the same way one does when trying to swim upstream to the source.

When they played that evening in Jajce, he hadn't drank. He still blew as hard, but didn't dance. He felt sullen and a bit raw. But he had caught the attention of a young woman. Although they didn't share a fluent common language, they shared scraps of French, German and a kind of hashed Slavic tongue. She took him by the hand after the concert and they walked into the evening. She showed him where the plums grew best, where they were almost ready for picking. He thought about leading them to a bar, but she insisted on sitting near the river and playing with words through a translator she had on her phone. She said the game was called *Shaskabiti*.

She explained that she had inherited it from her great-great-grandmother. Her family had lived and worked in Sarajevo, owning a tea-house near the riverbank. As a child she witnessed people from all over the world pass through the city, often trying to stammer their way towards an understanding through unfamiliar words.

As her great-great-grandmother grew a little older, she took on more responsibilities, talking with the guests and waiting on the patrons. She once found herself at a table with three strangers; one from China, one from Sweden and one from Slovenia. There were three different pots of tea on her tray.

There was a charged silence at the table as she arrived, then a confusing rush of questions as they tried to figure out which tea belonged to which person. As the words wove together around her and she struggled to explain it was all a mint tea with juniper berries, she heard three words fall side by side that provoked a strange, fresh sensation within her. *Sha* from the Chinese guest, *Ska* from the Swede and *Biti* from the Slovenian.

She whispered *Shaskabiti* and the three guests fell silent, long enough for her to place the tea in front of them. They all soon realised it was the same kind of tea and laughter encircled the table.

She adopted this word, uttering it whenever she needed a way through the different distant dialects. From there it took on meanings of its own as other people heard her say it and spoke it themselves beyond the tea house. In her family, it became synonymous with accepting or challenging fate as they attended to the delightful and deceitful guests.

Peter listened to her story and agreed to play, the new word feeling simultaneously familiar and alien. They sat for a long while beneath a plum tree blending words together, at times giggling, laughing at each other's pronunciation of words.

Out of curiosity, he typed the three words seperately into the translator; *sha* into Chinese, *ska* into Swedish and *biti* into Slovene.

Peter shivered as he stared at the phone in his hand. When read together, it roughly translated as *what shall be.*

They said it out loud to each other. He sensed something peculiar shifting within every time she said it to him, whilst looking into his eyes. They kissed, a brief kiss on each-others cheeks, and she asked him to walk her home. He did, then went to find the band.

The day of his birthday they arrived early in Sarajevo. They were playing in one of the street tents on Branilica Sarajeva, as part of the International Film Festival. On the drive to the city, he had convinced himself, and Cecil, that he wanted to change his name to Peter Shaskabiti. Cecil agreed, somehow hoping that it may also lead to another sober concert. They parked up and loaded the instruments into a container for equipment beside the stage and the beer stands. When they'd finished loading and the heat of the morning had begun to rise, he left them to go for a walk.

He spent most of the day up at the white fortress. He watched over the city, waiting for the evening to come. He heard the call of the muezzins, the tow and pull of the city traffic, the laughter of tourists climbing in and out of the windows to walk on the outer walls of the dilapidated fortress. He watched the city move below, separate from it all. The distance was enticing; he felt like a sultan of the Ottoman empire, his imagination lording over the movement of the city. He sat on a while longer.

A group of teenagers from Kovaci crawled through the stonework onto the ramparts. They didn't see Peter sat there and they carried on with their conversation.

"Yeah, I saw him too. What an idiot, just sleeping in the middle of the path like a dead horse!"

"Did you see the stains?"

"Yeah, like the gums of that guy from Ciglane in Gymnasium Park."

"Uh, they were all gluey and gummy brown. It was disgusting."

"Did you see the one who was so drunk he couldn't even get the bottle to his lips?"

"Ha, yeah, like watching someone juggling birds of sand."

He sat and listened to the teenagers. They kicked about up there all day. Peter remained hidden the whole time. It wasn't until the call of the Maghrib Salat that Peter was stirred free his reveries. The teenagers had gone. He was left alone on the stone wall. He walked down slowly through the streets, past the cemetery for the martyrs, the copper smiths with their coffee sets, the tourists with their chatter and stumble, washing over the old districts like a diseased blanket.

He got to the container and found the band getting ready. That night he dove off the stage with such fervour and passion. He danced without dropping a note. No one swung for him, he swung for no one. The band leader kept an eye on him, but seeing that he wasn't staggering let him carry on. He danced and two-stepped through the tables, leading the dancers through the dullards and mixing them together, all spinning like dervishes. He climbed back on stage to finish the set with the Orkestra.

The band leader, the famous Cecil Zupančič, came over to him as the other members carried an embellished Roma traditional and whispered in his ear.

"Are you ready now?"

Peter nodded, with his trombone still raised, his arm working furiously, sweat pouring out of him. Cecil turned to his Orkestra, arms raised and with a flick of his wrists there was a sudden silence on stage. A beat, two, three. The tension was incredible and then a scream went up from within him,

"NOW, SHASKABITI!"

And with that the stage erupted. Peter blew out a solo as clear as the water of the Soca and as rich as the hills on the Virsic Pass and as wild as the face of the Triglav. And he didn't stop. I don't think he could have, even if he tried.

Intermission for ears

I wonder where you wander in your thoughts when you consider music. How far along your ear canal does a melody swim before it becomes a dream? Is a sound a part of life breathing into us?

I wonder do you take care of your auricles?

Do you remember how to open them, to focus on the enchanting songs instead of the mantras of machination? And if not music then the songs of other species. Do you remember how to listen?

Did anyone ever teach you how to attend aurally to our world?

Are they open enough to allow life to transform you?

I wonder, can you feel the reverberations without relying on them? How does that feel? What else can you sense that I cannot?

Upon which rhythm does the hammer fall? Discordant or resonant?

I wonder whether what you hear suits your equilibrium. I wonder how we decide what is our sense of balance.

Is the pressure on either side of the tympanic membrane bearable? Are you sure it doesn't feel like drowning through the sky? Is your cochlea content?

I wonder what was the first sound you heard, or first vibration you felt?

I wonder, what may be the last?

I wonder what sounds soothe you, what arouse and amuse you?

Would you tell me? Would you whisper into my ear?

I wonder.

Resume

16   *Will you allow me the pleasure of disappearing?*

I imagine you looking at me as we arrive in Piazza Bellini. Perhaps I have overdone it. Perhaps. I do have a habit of talking a lot. But I needed to today. I needed that. I am relieved for now. I also know I need to leave soon. Maybe you've sensed it, maybe you were listening. The light returns to the street.

I devise so many variations of this moment, of parting ways, that I walk in silence as they play out. Some repeat. Others pass by only once. All fleeting. I stop.

I conjure up the courage to take up your hand in mine. It feels welcomed. I am relieved.

I cannot join you further into this night. I have a feeling that I need to go. A train to catch. A friend to meet up there, in the North. Will you allow me the pleasure of disappearing? That way, yes, I'll go through the portico in a moment. I want to say goodbye to an old friend.

–

I see you. I long to thank you for your company.

–

Thank you.

Until next we meet.

17   *Can you see their faces?*

I watch you walk your way, the tendrils of connection slowly unravelling themselves, returning to me rejuvenated and in need of a sleep. I'll sit here a to pull myself together.

Here, a habit. I wish to hold my breath; gather it up inside, fill up my diaphragm, fill up my lungs and then close my mouth. To adopt the seated Harpo Marx position, throw one leg over another, and watch the people moving about. To ponder after them all. To dream of them as they arrive before my eyes. Dressed in fantastic colours and the old fashions, dug out of the caves and tombs of Via Pugliana near Scavi Ercolana. What a brilliant mess of colour there is here.

People go flying about in all manner of moods and postures. What a delicious evening this is to be, a salacious moment to witness. Look at their faces. They are vibrant and in motion. I have no interest in whether they are drunk or not. What does it matter? You can never drink enough to compete with the mixture of Naples and twilight. Never. You'd be a fool or traumatised to even dare to try.

I feel the air slide from below to my lungs. My thoughts start to tighten. As if someone else was lacing my dancing shoes. If I wore dancing shoes, where would I be now? But no, not now.

As the air leaves me, as if by osmosis, pouring out through closed lips, I feel the delightful sense of mischief stoke my desire to shout something into the throng. To express my wonder. But what word could I shout?

What can we utter in the face of such good humour?

The air is almost gone now. Of its own natural accord, it seeks to expire. One cannot live on inspiration alone. Generations fostered on perpetual inspiration all struggling to breathe. Perhaps, I ought to breathe out, perhaps we ought to breathe out. To express; to expire. To let ancient ideas of control and power die. And to no longer resurrect them. To tell stories of *satyagraha*. To enact an alternative. To alter the narrative. Perhaps. And it would be such a misfortune to suffocate from inspiration in Piazza Bellini.

Have we forgotten how to expire? How many threads does this answer have?

Perhaps later I'll light a candle, allow the entrancing flame to stretch and shimmer. The dance of the smoke, the innocent trance. The rising scent of finality. Watching the flame. A moment to consider the death of the day. A space to grow accustomed to the anxiety before change. A little practice to keep the magnitude in balance.

A space to breathe it all out, to relinquish all that has been for all that could be. A relief.

Epilogue

I arrive in Piazza Dante and see that bloody clock again. I reach into my breast pocket to retrieve my ticket. A sigh. Only a brief sojourn from the journey onward, eleven hours of life curtailed by another train. I tuck the ticket inside again. This will be a fun sprint. I hustle myself towards the plinth that supports a stony resemblance of old, dead Dante. I push my palm to the stone, preparing to whisper an oath, a paraphrased avowal.

It's a secret. But I would never leave you here alone. Hope, yet, fills us; despair evades us still.

I whisper the word *remember* in as many tongues as I have acquired. I let go. I lean back, I could fall. I adore this moment, the crest of realisation; gravity is shifting; the planet is rolling and I with it. I pivot. I dream a childhood dream of being a ballet dancer. I let the longing to live *en l'air* pour through me and into my feet. I cannot help but smile, a little silliness is remedy enough to transform the anguish into joy.

I whisper to the wind:

To each new day we take new steps,

Some big, some small,

But none shall we forget.

And as each day ends,

find a new way home

with eager, tired steps.

Some big, some small,

But none shall we forget.

I begin my departure with an adagio through the people of the square, humming the tune to myself. I consider my desires, the heft of my body. I imagine the buoyancy necessary to dance me through the people on the streets between me and the station. By the time I get to the cobbles of Piazza Bellini for the last time I am free of ballast, a comedy of small and large leaps, assemblé and flying brisé and cabriole.

One has to elaborate on their humour somehow. One must remember there is always enough time for change.

I'm still laughing by the time I take my seat on the twilight train. Gladdened by the age of the carriage and the tables, the windows that open. It will be a long, slow journey north. I settle into my seat and retrieve the deck of cards from my pocket. I shuffle. I lay out the peculiar array to practice.

"What's that?" I hear a lady ask me in a language I recognise.

"Welsh Solitaire."

"Don't know it. Fancy a game?"

I turn to face the questioner and find a woman holding a double bass beside the table. She slings a holdall onto the rack above us and supports the neck of the instrument as she wriggles into the seat opposite me. With care and ease she hauls the bass into the aisle seat. She leans the instrument over a little and returns her attention to the cards.

"Where are you off to?" I ask as I reshuffle the cards, preparing the crude half deck for each of us.

"Slovenia," she replies, accepting the cards.

"Likewise," and I begin to explain the game as the train lurches onward.

Acknowledgements

I wish to acknowledge and offer a heartfelt thanks to all the people who helped raise the printing costs for *Witness* and extend my sincere gratitude to:

Siân, Anthony and Josh Moon; Mark and Karen Holton; Audrey Holton; Shaun and Amanda Dilks; Benita Bock, Benna and Trevor Baker; Alex, Charlotte, Nye and Manny Upham; Dai and Sue Jones; Rebecca King; Billy Hanwell and Lara Graßl.

Thank you.